Beetle and Lulu

Beetle and Friends

**Get together with Beetle
and his friends!**

Be sure to read:
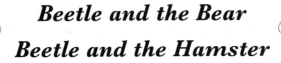
Beetle and the Bear
Beetle and the Hamster

... and lots, lots more!

Beetle and Lulu

Hilary McKay
illustrated by Lesley Harker

■SCHOLASTIC

To Bella, with love – H.M.

Scholastic Children's Books,
Commonwealth House, 1-19 New Oxford Street,
London, WC1A 1NU, UK
a division of Scholastic Ltd
London ~ New York ~ Toronto ~ Sydney ~ Auckland
Mexico City ~ New Delhi ~ Hong Kong

First published by Scholastic Ltd, 2002

ISBN 0 439 98101 8

Printed and bound by Oriental Press, Dubai, UAE

10 9 8 7 6 5 4 3 2 1

Chapter One

There was a boy in Beetle's class called
Harvey. He was a lot bigger than Beetle.
He wore a black baseball cap pulled on
backwards. He used his cap like a frisbee
to flip at people.

Harvey used to tease Beetle a lot.
He thought Beetle's hair
was very funny.

He would pull it and say, "Hey Beetle,
you need a haircut! You look like one
of the girls!"

Beetle would mutter, "Leave my hair
alone!" and go bright,
bright red.

One day Harvey found
a pink sparkly hair clip
on the classroom floor.

It was a hot
afternoon. Sunlight
poured in through
the windows getting
in people's eyes and making it hard to
think. Everyone was half asleep. It was
easy for Harvey to wander past Beetle's
chair and sneak the hair clip into
Beetle's hair.

Nobody noticed until Harvey called out,
"Hey Beetle, that looks cool!"

Then everyone looked at Beetle and even
Mrs Holiday, the class teacher, laughed.

Beetle grabbed the hair clip out of his hair
and threw it hard
at Harvey.

The clip hit Lulu by mistake.

"It didn't hurt a bit," said Lulu, who lived
next door to Beetle and was Beetle's friend.

"It might have done," said Mrs Holiday, and she made Beetle stand on one side of the classroom and Harvey on the other, where she could see what they were doing.

"It has been a long, hot day," she said. "Thank goodness it is nearly over."

✏ Chapter Two ✏

As soon as school finished, Beetle rushed
outside. Harvey was right behind him.
He flipped his baseball cap at Beetle's head
and said, "Just like one of the girls!" He
only stopped doing it when he saw Beetle's
big brother Max coming towards him.

When Beetle got home he said, "I want
my hair cut off. All of it. Right off."

Beetle's mother said, "Oh no! You have
lovely hair. You will just look old and tough
if you have it all cut short!"

"I want to look old and tough," said Beetle.

Beetle's mother laughed and ruffled Beetle's hair. "It's going all gold in the sunshine," she said.

Max tried to help Beetle. He said, "That's not going gold, Mum. That's fading. Beetle's hair is so old it's fading."

"Rubbish," said Beetle's mother.

Beetle went away and thought at the
end of the garden. Lulu watched him from
over the fence.

Beetle said, "It's my hair. *I* grew it. I can
do what I like with it."

"What are you going to do?" asked Lulu.

"You'll see," said Beetle.

He went inside and secretly borrowed his mother's sewing scissors.

Then he went back down the garden and cut large chunks of hair off all over his head.

Lulu pushed back her own long curls and said, "You're doing the right thing, Beetle. It's much too hot for long hair."

Chapter Three

The next day was Saturday and it was still very hot. Beetle's mother grumbled a lot about having to go into town with Beetle to get his hair cut properly.

"You have to," said Lulu. "Poor Beetle can't go about like that."

"I loved Beetle's curls," said Beetle's mother, and to Beetle she said, "Lulu has ten times more hair than you do, and she puts up with it, don't you Lulu?"

"Hmm," said Lulu.

Just after Beetle and his mother got to the hairdresser's somebody else arrived.

Harvey.

"Beetle!" said Harvey's mother, and "Harvey!" said Beetle's mother, and they spoke in pleased voices, just as if Harvey and Beetle were best friends.

Beetle and Harvey did not say a word to each other. They sat in chairs side by side with a hairdresser each and glared at each other's reflections in the mirror.

Beetle's hairdresser said, "Are you boys friends, then?"

"NO!" said Beetle and Harvey.

The two hairdressers looked at each other and laughed.

Beetle's hair was finished first. His hairdresser showed him the back of his head in a mirror.

"What do you think of that?" he asked.

Beetle glanced across at Harvey's reflection and said, "I'd like it shorter please."

Then Harvey was finished.

He looked at Beetle.

"Much shorter please," he said.

More hair came off Beetle's head.

More hair came off Harvey's.

"Shorter still, if you don't mind," said
Beetle, when the scissors stopped once more.

"I don't mind," said the hairdresser.

"Anything you say!"

"Much, much shorter," said Harvey, a minute or two later. "Can't you buzz it all off with a razor? I don't want to look like a girl!"

Hair fell from Beetle and Harvey like itchy rain.

Suddenly Beetle's mother looked up and saw what Beetle looked like.

"Oh no, Beetle!" she screamed.

Harvey laughed.

Beetle's mother made Beetle get off his chair straight away.

Out in the market place she bought him a baseball cap to stop him getting sunstroke.

Beetle had never had such short hair in his life. It was so short that when he took the cap off he could feel the sunlight pouring straight into his brain.

Chapter Four

When they got home Max was out at a
friend's house, so Beetle wandered out into
the garden. Lulu was having a girls-only
party in the garden next door. The girls
climbed up the fence to have a look at Beetle.

Beetle showed them how he could stick his
head in a bucket of cold water and come
up and shake himself
dry in seconds.

He let them try on his baseball cap and
he told them about the lovely feeling of
sunlight pouring into
his brain.

Lulu looked longingly at the bucket of cold water. She pulled her thick black curls and said, "I wish I had short hair."

"I could go and get Mum's scissors," offered Beetle.

Lulu looked at Beetle to see if he was joking.

Then she said to all the girls at her party,
"Don't dare say a word!" and she climbed
over the fence.

There was a great gasp from the girls
when Beetle made the first cut. He paused,
with his scissors in the air.

"Carry on," said Lulu calmly.

Beetle cut all the hair off the top of Lulu's head. Then all the hair from the sides.

"Lean forward," he ordered, and he cut all the hair from the back.

Lulu ran her fingers over her head.

She sprinkled it
with water from
Beetle's bucket.

She pranced
around the garden
letting the sunshine
pour into her brain.
"It feels lovely!"
she said.

Abbie, Lulu's
cousin, scrambled over
the fence and said, "I want mine done too."

Lulu cut off Abbie's hair for her, and as soon as she put down the scissors, Georgia climbed over and grabbed them.

"I need them next," said Rachel.

Then the great hair cutting began. Beetle went into the house for more scissors and they cut off Georgia's plaits and Rachel's bunches.

They sheared Samantha's curls and Amanda's ponytail.

Then they started on Kerstin's ginger hair.
Everyone was very excited and cheerful
except Laura and Melly.

Laura and Melly said they were going
to tell.

"Don't tell until they've done mine too!"
Emma begged.

Laura and Melly waited while they did
Kerstin and Emma.

Then they sniffed unhappily and said, "Everyone always leaves us out of everything!"

So Beetle and Lulu cut Laura and Melly's hair too, and they were careful to cut it very short, so that Laura and Melly should not feel at all left out.

Then Max arrived home and he came
running down the garden in search of
Beetle, just as Lulu's mother called, "Girls,
girls, where have you
got to? Time to
go home."

One after another the girls climbed back over the fence and disappeared. Max stood with his mouth open, watching them go.

"Crikey, Beetle!" he said. "I think there's going to be trouble."

Max was right. Moments later screams started coming from Lulu's house.

✏ Chapter Five ✏

Although it was half past five on a hot
Saturday afternoon Beetle decided to go
to bed. In bed he tried very hard to go
to sleep before anyone should think of
coming to talk to him.

But it did not work. Before the day was
over he had been told off by eleven sets
of parents, including his own.

"I wonder what Harvey will say,"
chuckled Max late that night when the last
telling off was over.

"I'd forgotten about Harvey,"
said Beetle sleepily.

Harvey was waiting at the school gates for Beetle on Monday morning. All that was left of Harvey's hair now was a sort of brownish haze around his head.

Harvey reached out and tweaked Beetle's baseball cap away and said, "Hey Beetle, you want to get a haircut! You look just like..."

Then Harvey stopped speaking and his mouth fell open. He was staring at something behind Beetle.

Beetle turned round to look too, and there was Lulu, and all the girls from Lulu's party. They looked very pleased with themselves, and they were all wearing back to front baseball caps.

They pulled off their caps as they came
up to Beetle and Harvey. The girls had
been tidied up since Beetle last saw them,
and now their hair was even shorter.
Laura's and Melly's was the shortest of all.

"We had it all buzzed off with a razor!"
said Melly proudly.

Harvey's face was so funny that Beetle
could not stop laughing.

"Hey Harvey,"
said Lulu, "you look
just like one of the girls!"

Harvey went bright,
bright red.

Then Beetle and the girls ran off into the sunny playground, laughing and flipping baseball caps at each other like frisbees.

Harvey stood watching them, twisting his
cap in his hands. He seemed to be thinking.
He looked a bit lonely.

After a while Harvey seemed to decide
what to do, and he ran off after the others.
He hung around the edge of the laughing
crowd, until Beetle noticed him there, and
flipped a cap to him. Then
Harvey gave a sudden,
happy grin, and
flipped it back.